JE

Bradbury Press
Macmillan Publishing Company
866 Third Avenue
New York, NY 10022

Collier Macmillan Canada, Inc.
1200 Eglinton Avenue East
Suite 200
Don Mills, Ontario M3C 3N1

First published 1991 in Great Britain by Walker Books, Ltd.
First American edition 1991
Printed and bound in Hong Kong
10 9 8 7 6 5 4 3 2 1

Library of Congress Cataloging-in-Publication Data
Gliori, Debi.
New big sister / by Debi Gliori. — 1st American ed.
p.   cm.
Summary: A young girl describes her mother's pregnancy, from the
first bout of morning sickness to the joyful delivery of twins.
ISBN 0-02-735995-6
[1. Babies—Fiction. 2. Pregnancy—Fiction. 3. Brothers and
sisters—Fiction.] I. Title.
PZ7.G4889Ne 1991
[E]—dc20   90-49272

new BIG sister

DEBI GLIORI

Bradbury Press New York

Maxwell Macmillan International Publishing Group
New York Oxford Singapore Sydney

for Rowan and Benjamin with love

I heard Mom being sick in the
bathroom this morning.

I think Dad's got it too, because when
I told him about Mom, he looked a
bit ill. It's odd, though –

Mom went to the doctor about being
sick, but when she came out,
the doctor was smiling.

Dad's better now,

but Mom's off her food.

I asked Sophie if her mom was sick in
the mornings, and she said only
when she was having a baby.

I wonder what it's like having a baby.

I asked Mom at tea time. She told me
she *is* having a baby.

We all got so excited that we let the
toast burn.

Mom took a long time to grow a baby.
I had a birthday…

and our cat had four kittens, and we all
had Christmas!

Mom started to grow so big she
could hardly see her toes for her tummy.

She ate millions of marmalade and cold
spaghetti sandwiches.

When they went to the hospital
to have the baby,

Grandma stayed with me.

As soon as Dad told us the news, he
went to pick Mom flowers.

He said we'd go to the hospital
after supper. He was so tired he
fell asleep over his plate.

When we got to the hospital, we went
up to Mom's room.

She was sitting up in bed and she
looked very small.

In came the nurse with a baby.
"Here's your baby sister," she said.
The door opened again and...

in came the doctor with another baby.
"And here's your baby brother," he said.

Dad opened a bottle of very noisy
champagne and Mom said,
"To a new big sister."